For Elizabeth and Robert

First published in Great Britain 1987
by Hamish Hamilton Children's Books
This Magnet edition first published 1989
by Methuen Children's Books
A Division of the Octopus Group Ltd
Michelin House, 81 Fulham Road, London sw3 6rb
Text copyright © 1987 by Robert McCrum
Illustrations copyright © 1987 by Chris Riddell
Printed in Great Britain

isbn 416 09212 8

The
Dream Boat
BRONTOSAURUS

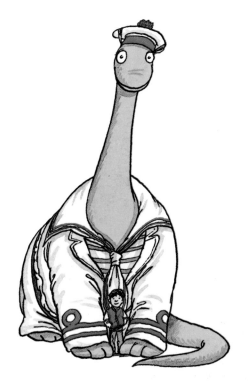

Robert McCrum

Illustrated by Chris Riddell

A Magnet Book

So the brontosaurus was a Superstar and *everyone* knew all about him. He was rich, famous and successful, and had all the hamburgers he wanted. But there was one big problem.

Nobody would leave him alone.

Every day coachloads of sightseers drove along Bobby's street for a glimpse of the celebrated monster.

'It's like living in a zoo,' complained Bobby's father, staring crossly back at a party of Japanese. 'This fossil's nothing but trouble.'

The brontosaurus, who was sitting outside the window eating the roses as usual, looked offended. 'Don't mind my dad, prehistoric partner,' said Bobby. 'It's just his way of saying he loves you.'

The next day, when Bobby came down to breakfast, there was a letter next to his cornflakes. He recognised the paleolithic handwriting.

Dear Boby, i ve gon too
Look for a bit of peec and
quite. Perhapps ill find
anuther monster. Pleez dont
worry aboat mee. ill be bak
Sun, yor frend, B.

'Spelling was never his strong point,' said Bobby's mother.

'I wonder what he's up to?' said Liz, Bobby's sister.

'One monster's more than enough for me,' said his father.

Bobby smiled to himself. He knew that whenever the brontosaurus disappeared there was always an adventure on the way.

He was right, of course. A few days later, there was a noise in the street. Bobby rushed outside and there was his megalithic companion wearing an amazing sailor suit.

'What's all this about?' asked Bobby, pointing to his clothes.

The brontosaurus gave a wink. Then with a swish of his long scaly tail he planted Bobby on his back and began to run faster . . . FASTER . . . *FASTER*.

'I didn't know you could fly,' said Bobby.

Suddenly they were at the seaside. The sun was shining. And there, in the middle of the bay, was the finest yacht Bobby had ever seen. Painted in huge gold letters on the stern was its name: *Brontosaurus*.

'You always did have a big ego,' said Bobby affectionately.

The brontosaurus gave his friend a look that said: Are you ready for an adventure? Was he ready? He couldn't wait!

First they met the captain, who was a chimpanzee.

'Haven't I seen you before somewhere?' asked Bobby.

'Och, aye,' replied the captain, a wrinkly old Scot. 'I'm from the zoo. Me and the brontosaurus are old acquaintances.'

'And so are we!' chorused a couple of voices behind him.

Suddenly a couple of smaller chimpanzees in tartan kilts popped up 'We're the McChimps,' they said with one voice. 'We used to work at McDonalds. That's how we know the brontosaurus.'

The brontosaurus smiled at the McChimps approvingly.

The *Brontosaurus* was a fabulous sailing boat. There was a saloon with a bar. There was a ballroom with its own orchestra. There was an indoor swimming pool, a private cinema and a helipad. The bedroom was the size of Bobby's house.

'Fan—tastic,' said Bobby.

'What kind of a boat can this be?' Bobby asked.
  'It's a DREAM BOAT,' said the McChimps in unison.
  'What's a dream boat?' asked Bobby.
  'Look!' said the McChimps, turning him towards the shore.
  Bobby looked. The harbour and all the people had gone.

'Make your wish,' said the McChimps. 'Then the Dream Boat will take you on a trip.'

'Where to?'

'You won't know till you close your eyes,' said the McChimps.

Bobby closed his eyes and made an *enormous* wish. He began to feel drowsy and he knew he was drifting off to sleep . . . .

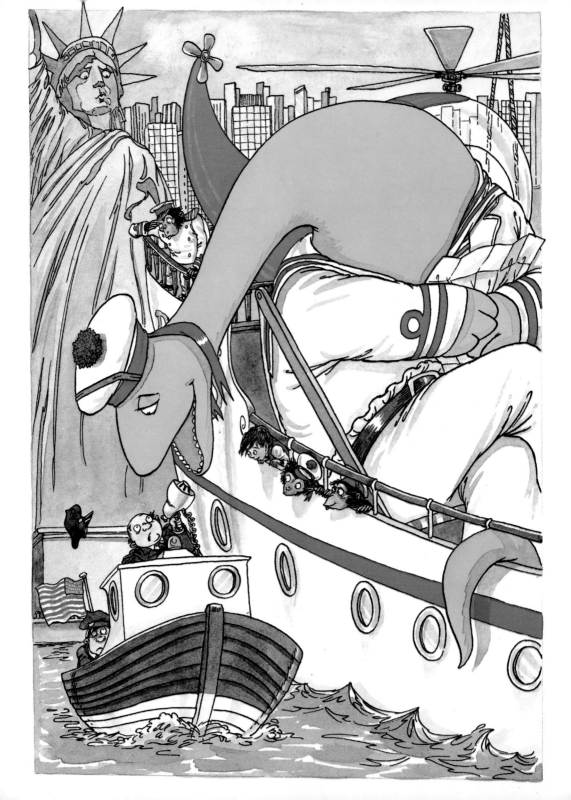

When he opened his eyes Bobby was not sure where he was. He thought he could hear the sound of the McChimps having an argument.

He pulled on his clothes and ran up on deck.

The brontosaurus was sitting in a deck-chair holding a map.

'Hoots, man, we're way off course,' said the McChimps. 'We set the compass wrong. We're supposed to be in the Caribbean.'

'So where are we, actually?' asked Bobby.

'Actually, we're in New York, dumbo,' said the McChimps. 'Don't you know anything?' they groaned. 'Look!'

There behind him was the Statue of Liberty.

As they spoke, a motor-boat with a fat customs officer came alongside.

'Where ya from?' he asked. 'And what's ya business?'

The brontosaurus opened his mouth wide in a yawn. The customs man went white. 'No offence, buster. Just doing my dooty.'

'Time for a change of scene,' said the McChimps. 'Shut your eyes, Bobby.'

Bobby shut his eyes. 'Watch that map,' he shouted.

'Count to ten!' cried the McChimps.

Bobby began to count. ONE, TWO, THREE, FOUR, FIVE . . . The wind rushed through his hair. He felt the Dream Boat gathering speed.

SIX, SEVEN, EIGHT . . . Everything went very still.

NINE, TEN.

'Ten!' said Bobby out loud.

'Open your eyes,' shouted the McChimps.

Bobby opened his eyes and gasped. The Dream Boat was moored next to the greenest tropical island he had ever seen. The sound of steel drums floated across the water.

Bobby and the brontosaurus had the best holiday of their lives. They drank coconut milk and Coca-Cola. The brontosaurus even got a sun-tan.

'Was it like this in the good old days?' Bobby asked. 'I mean before the Ice Age?'

The brontosaurus nodded his head sadly.

'Wouldn't it be terrific if we could leave him behind?' Bobby suggested to the McChimps. 'He hasn't had it so good for centuries!'

'But you don't understand,' they said. 'It's only a dream.'

'Sometimes dreams come true,' Bobby replied. 'Mine did. I dreamed the brontosaurus was real. And he was.'

'Och, man, that was in the real world. This is the Dream Boat. Things are always changing on the Dream Boat. Close your eyes and you'll see!'

The landscape began to shake and rumble. The leaves fell off the trees. The beaches turned white. It became incredibly cold. They were in the Antarctic.

The brontosaurus sat in his cabin reading *The Beano*, shivering and drinking hot chocolate. 'You don't like this, do you?' said Bobby. 'It reminds you of the Ice Age.'

The brontosaurus was beginning to look rather unwell.

'Help!' cried Bobby. 'The brontosaurus won't survive if we stay in this climate.'

The McChimps scratched their heads. 'We're working on it, man. Chill out!'

'Can't you have another dream?' said Bobby.

'We're dreamin', Bobby,' they said. 'We're dreamin'.'

The brontosaurus was already huddled under an enormous duvet. When the McChimps began to snore, Bobby fell asleep as well.

When he woke up it was warmer and the brontosaurus was munching a hamburger. He seemed much happier.

Bobby went out on deck. The Dream Boat was moored in a swimming pool inside a huge hall filled with every imaginable kind of craft.

'It's a Boat Show,' said Bobby with surprise.

He leant over the side and shouted to one of the visitors. 'Excuse me,' he said, 'but would you mind telling me where we are just now?'

The man looked astonished. 'This is Australia, mate. And don't you forget it.'

'Whose idea was *this*?' said Bobby turning to the McChimps.

'Not mine,' said the first. 'It's his. He's always wanted to go Down Under.'

Now a man in a pair of khaki shorts and a floppy hat appeared on deck.

'Good day, mate,' he said. 'Mind if I step aboard?' The name's Bruce. Who's your friend?'

'That's the world-famous brontosaurus. He's come to look at Australia.'

'Fair dinkum,' said Bruce. 'Nice boat you have here. Does she race?'

Bobby said he didn't know. No one had ever tried.

'What class is she?'

'She's a Dream Boat.'

He pointed round the hall. 'These boats have come from all over the world to race here. Australia's got to win.'

The McChimps were excited. 'We'll sail it for you.'

Bruce looked unhappy. 'If I ship a couple of apes on board – no offence, mind you – I'll be the laughing stock of Australia,' he said.

'No chimps, no Dream Boat,' said Bobby. 'If you lose, you'll be the laughing stock, too.'

Bruce gulped. 'Okay,' he said. He looked at the brontosaurus. 'Will zoo features want to come along too?'

'Now there's no need to be rude,' said Bobby firmly. 'We're all coming.'

Soon they had the best rooms in the best hotel in Australia, and the brontosaurus had all the kangarooburgers he could possibly want.

The day of the race came. There were yachts from all over the world: France, New Zealand, America, Italy and England.

All the spectators were very excited. The Dream boat *Brontosaurus* flew the Australian flag. Bruce, Bobby and the brontosaurus were up bright and early.

It was Bobby who noticed that the McChimps were missing.

Bobby and the brontosaurus rushed off to the hotel. The McChimps were jumping up and down at the window.

'This is dirty work at the crossroads,' said Bobby. 'They're locked in. Now we're done for. Unless . . . .'

When he woke up, he was shivering. The McChimps were leaping about the cabin with bowls of porridge. Bobby wiped the steam off the porthole. 'Scotland, of course,' he said. 'No wonder those two are so happy.'

They sailed down the coast and they all sang 'Over the sea to Skye'. The McChimps visited all their friends and relations and ate lots of porridge.

One morning, Bobby woke to find the brontosaurus missing.

'He's been out all night,' said the McChimps. They winked. 'He's found a friend.'

There was a strange splashing sound outside. They all went on deck. It was very misty. But they could just make out the shape of the brontosaurus swimming through the water. And at his side was a SECOND monster.

The McChimps were very excited. 'Don't tell us!' they shouted. 'We know who *she* is. She's called Nessie.'

'Welcome aboard, errant fossils,' said Bobby.

He looked at his watch. 'Time to be on our way,' he said. He wondered what his father would say when he arrived with *two* monsters.

So they tied the Dream Boat *Brontosaurus* up in the harbour and came
home to the little house on the edge of the big city.

Everyone was very glad to see them and to hear about all the
adventures on the Dream Boat.

'So now he'll be eating my roses again,' said Bobby's father. 'Well,
thank goodness there's only one of him.'

'Oh,' said Bobby. 'Did I forget to tell you?'

'What's that? What's that?'

'Er . . . well . . . he's found a friend.'

'He . . . A what, a WHAT ! ! ! A friend ! ! I don't believe it,' exclaimed
his father, jumping out of his chair.

And there in the garden, side by side with Nessie, was the brontosaurus, eating the roses as usual.

'I think this is a dream,' muttered Bobby's father.

'Perhaps it is,' said Bobby cheerfully. 'Wait till you find the chimpanzees in the garage.'

'Time for bed,' said his mother. 'Really, you do tell the tallest stories sometimes, Bobby.'

Bobby smiled. So did the brontosaurus. And so did Nessie.

They know that all *their* stories are true.

The Surfing Wallaby Hotel

They rushed back to the Dream Boat just in time for the start of the race. Bruce pretended to be a brilliant navigator, but Bobby and the McChimps knew they had their work cut out. They closed their eyes and made a wish . . . and the Dream Boat swept ahead of all the other yachts in the race.

There were loud cheers as it crossed the line first. BOOM! went the finishing gun.

Bruce was delighted. 'It's a dream come true,' he said proudly.

The sea air had made them all sleepy. Bobby curled up next to the brontosaurus and fell asleep just like that.